Dayaxa ayaa ila lugeeyaya xalay.
Sida waraaqda la duuliyo ama kaytka ayuu i daba socday,

Though there wasn't a string or a tail in sight
when I took the Moon for a walk.

Laakiin xadhig iyo hoggaan midna kumaan jiidin
markii Dayaxu ila lugeeyay.

I carried my blue torch just in case
the Moon got scared and hid its face.

Tooshkaygii buluugga ahaa ayaan iska sii qaatay
Dayaxii ayaa baqay oo wejigiisa qariyay.

Laakiin marba daruuraha khafiifka ah
ayuu ka soo dhex baxaayay
Markii Dayaxu ila lugeeyay.

But it peeked through clouds
that were fragile as lace
When I took the Moon for a walk.

I warned the Moon to rise a bit higher
so it wouldn't get hooked on a church's tall spire,

Dayaxii ayaan u digay in uu sare u yara kaco
si aanu kaniisadda saqafkeeda u jiidhin,

While the neighbourhood dogs made a train-whistle choir
when I took the Moon for a walk.

Xilligaas eeyda xaafadda ayaa mar wada ciyaayay sidii tareenka hoonkiisa markii Dayaxu ila lugeeyay.

We tiptoed through grass where the night crawlers creep
when the rust-bellied robins have all gone to sleep,

Waxaannu dhex cidhibsannay cawska halka cayayaanku habeenkii dhex xamaartaan
xilligaas oo xitaa shimbiruhu seexdeen.

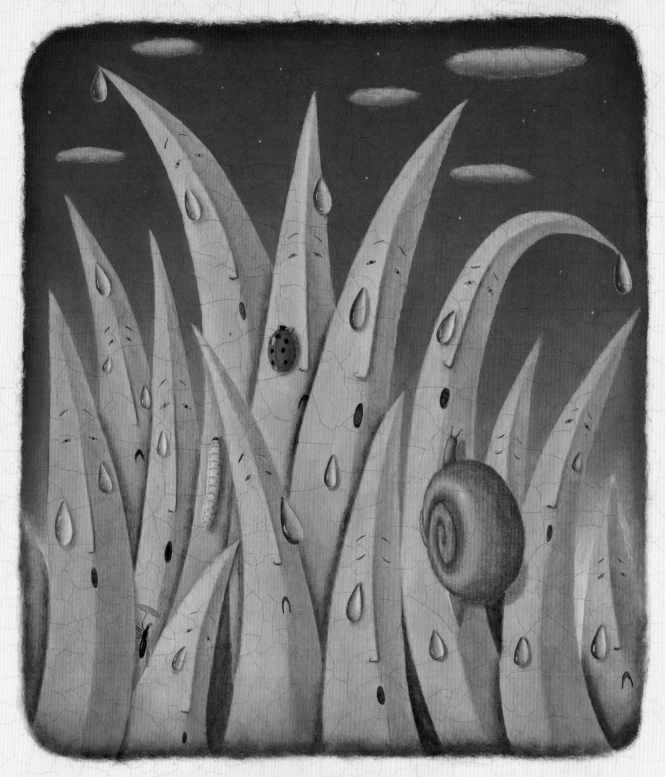

Markaasaa Dayaxu u yeedhay sayaxa korka saaran cawskana la
mooday inuu ilmaynaayo
Markii Dayaxu ila lugeeyay.

And the Moon called the dew so the grass seemed to weep
When I took the Moon for a walk.

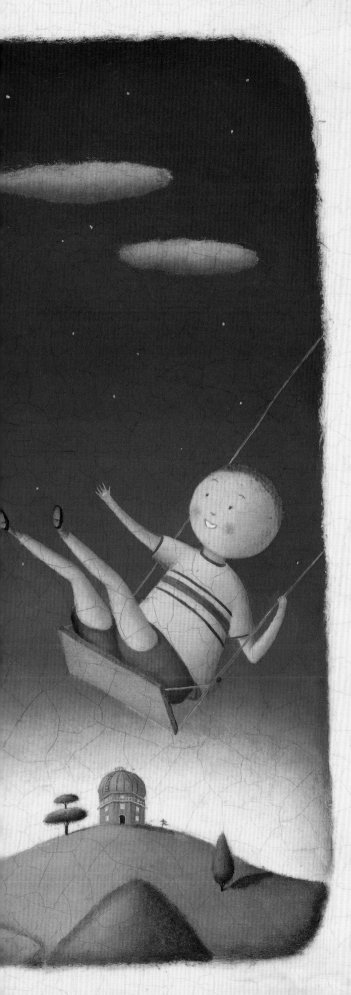

Markaasaannu leexada u tartannay oo
aan lugahayga sare u taagay halkaas
oo aan u maleeyay in Dayaxu igu
yidhi duul,

We raced for the swings,
where I kicked my feet high
And imagined the Moon had
just asked me to fly,

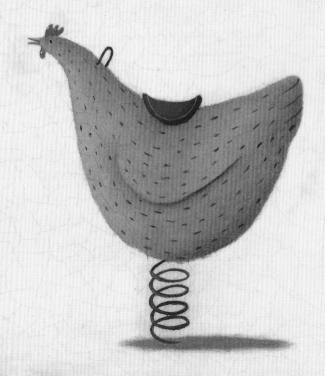

Hand holding hand through the starry night sky
when I took the Moon for a walk.

Iyada oo gacaniba gacan haysato oo aannu cirka habeenkii ee xiddigaha
leh dhex duulayno,
markii Dayaxu ila lugeeyay.

We danced 'cross the bridge where the smooth waters flow.
The Moon was above and the Moon was below,

Markaasaannu biriishka halka biyihu hoos maraan cayaar kaga gudubnay.
Dayaxu korka ayuu joogay haddana Dayaxu hoosta ayuu ka muuqday,

Markaasaan labadoodii is dhex taagay oo labada dhinacba ka dhalaalayay markii Dayaxu ila lugeeyay.

And bright in between them
I echoed in their glow
When I took the Moon for a walk.

Then as we turned back, the Moon kept me in sight.
It followed me home and stayed there all night,

Markaasaannu dib u noqonnay, Dayaxuna weli isii eegayay.
Illaa gurigii ayuu isii dabagalay oo halkii taagnaa habeenkii oo dhan,

And thanked me by sharing its sweet sleepy light
when I took the Moon for a walk.

Oo wuu ii mahadceliyay inaan la wadaagay iftiinkiisa khafiifka ah
ee wanaagsan
markii Dayaxu ila lugeeyay.

The Mysterious Moon

What do you see when you look at the moon? Children who live in Europe and the United States imagine that they see a man when they look at the moon. Children in Japan and India see a rabbit, and children in Australia see a kitten. But all children, no matter where they live, look up in wonder at the same moon.

The moon is primarily made of rock with a small iron core. It creates no light of its own, but reflects sunlight.

The shape of the moon seems to change during the month because the sunlight strikes the moon at different angles as it travels through space. These shapes are called 'phases'. Here are some of the phases of the moon:

New Moon   *Crescent Moon*   *Half Moon*   *Gibbous Moon*   *Full Moon*

When the moon is growing larger in the sky, we say that it is 'waxing'. When it is growing smaller, we say that it is 'waning'.

For people all over the world, the moon has always been an important way to measure time. Although the solar calendar has become the standard international way of doing this, many people still use lunar, or moon, calendars.

The moon can be a friend to farmers and gardeners - those who follow tradition know that the best time to sow seeds and transplant young shoots is when the moon is waxing.

Moon festivals are celebrated in many societies. The Chinese Moon Festival is held during the Harvest Moon - the full moon that rises in mid-autumn.

Many Celtic and Native American festivals are also held at the time of the Harvest Moon, when the people give thanks for the harvest and for all living things on earth.

The World at Night

If you took the moon for a walk through your neighbourhood, what would you show it? What would you hear, and what would you see?

Wherever you are, you would probably see some nocturnal creatures - mammals, birds and insects that usually sleep during the day and come out at night. They are especially adapted to life under the moon and stars:

Cats have eyes that see very well in the dark.

Rabbits have large ears that capture sound across long distances.

Bats use sounds and echoes to help them fly safely and find food.

Fireflies light up at night so that they can find each other.

Owls have necks that can turn right around and huge, flat eyes that enable them to see other creatures that are far away.

Some flowers are nocturnal too. They bloom and release their fragrance after dark.

And although you are asleep during the night, your mind is not! During the day, your waking, or conscious, mind is active, but when you sleep, your dreaming, or unconscious, mind is busy. So, the world at night is not so quiet as it seems!

For my nephew Christopher, *who first walked with the moon*
and my mother Estella, *who held his hand*
For my father Harold, *the star we steer by*
and Lucan, *my sun*
and, of course, for Emilie, *for Everything* - C.C.

The author extends heartfelt thanks to the society of Children's Book Writers and Illustrators for generous support in the form of
a Barbara Karlin Grant, WarmLines Parent Resources, Jane Yolen, the Jeff Kelly and Newton Library Critique Groups, and Alison Keehn.

For Mark, happy moon walking, love from Alison.

Mantra Lingua TalkingPEN
Global House
303 Ballards Lane
London N12 8NP
www.mantralingua.com
www.talkingpen.co.uk

First published in Great Britain in 2004 by Barefoot Books Ltd
Dual language edition first published 2008 by Mantra Lingua
This edition 2013

Printed in Hatfield,UK FP251013PB11133703

A CIP record of this book is available from the British Library